Five reasons why we think you'll love this book!

Winnie AND Wilbur
THE HAUNTED HOUSE

This story is full of spooktacular magic!

Learn how to say 'Abracadabra' . . . backwards!

There is so much to spot in every picture.

Can you find Wilbur hiding in an upstairs window?

You can take the Winnie and Wilbur challenge:
how many times can you spot the bee?

Freya

Anushka

Maggie

Bailey

Johannes

Molly

Ashley

Amber

Jun-Yeong

Pablo

Matilda

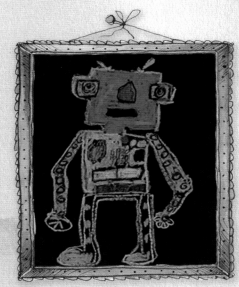

Marwin

Hasan

Rebecca

Thank you to all these schools for helping with the endpapers:

St Barnabas Primary School, Oxford; St Ebbe's Primary School, Oxford; Marcham Primary School, Abingdon; St Michael's C.E. Aided Primary School, Oxford; St Bede's RC Primary School, Jarrow; The Western Academy, Beijing, China; John King School, Pinxton; Neston Primary School, Neston; Star of the Sea RC Primary School, Whitley Bay; José Jorge Letria Primary School, Cascais, Portugal; Dunmore Primary School, Abingdon; Özel Bahçeşehir İlköğretim Okulu, Istanbul, Turkey; the International School of Amsterdam, the Netherlands; Princethorpe Infant School, Birmingham.

For Summer, Charlie and Miles—V.T.

For Zoe Tzannes—now every day
is a Zoe day!—K.P.

OXFORD
UNIVERSITY PRESS

Great Clarendon Street, Oxford OX2 6DP

Oxford University Press is a department of the University of Oxford. It furthers the University's objective of excellence in research, scholarship, and education by publishing worldwide. Oxford is a registered trade mark of Oxford University Press in the UK and in certain other countries

Text copyright © Valerie Thomas 2015
Illustrations copyright © Korky Paul 2015, 2016
The moral rights of the author and artist
have been asserted

Database right Oxford University Press (maker)

First published as *Winnie's Haunted House* in 2015
This edition first published in 2018

British Library Cataloguing in Publication Data available

ISBN: 978-0-19-277193-3 (paperback)

10 9 8 7 6 5 4 3 2 1

Printed in China

Paper used in the production of this book is a natural, recyclable product made from wood grown in sustainable forests. The manufacturing process conforms to the environmental regulations of the country of origin

www.winnieandwilbur.com

VALERIE THOMAS AND KORKY PAUL

Winnie AND Wilbur

THE HAUNTED HOUSE

OXFORD

UNIVERSITY PRESS

It was a lovely, warm,
sunny afternoon.
Winnie the Witch thought
she'd have a sleep.

She sat down in her big armchair,
shut her eyes, and in two minutes
she was snoring.

Wilbur, Winnie's big black cat,
thought he'd have a sleep, too.

He curled up on a cushion,
shut his eyes, and in three minutes . . .

a bumblebee flew in
through the window.

BuzzzZz!

Wilbur liked to chase bumblebees.
He jumped up at the bumblebee,

and missed.

He jumped up again . . . higher . . .

missed the bumblebee . . .

and landed . . .

in the big vase of flowers
on Winnie's table.

CRASH! SMASH! SPLASH!

Winnie woke up.
'Oh no! My best vase!' she said.
'Did you do that, Wilbur?'
But she couldn't see
Wilbur anywhere.

'Where are my glasses?'
asked Winnie.
'Who took them?'

She bent down to look for them.

Wilbur shot out from
under Winnie's chair.
Where could he hide?

Behind the curtains.

SWISH! CRASH!

Down came the curtains, on top of Winnie.

'Blithering broomsticks!'
she shouted.
Winnie crawled out from
under the curtains.
'Who did that? Was it a ghost?
Is my house haunted?'

Wilbur raced up the stairs.
Where could he hide?

Then he saw the perfect place.
Winnie would never look up there.

Wilbur jumped onto the banister
and then sprang onto the chandelier.

The chandelier swung
from side to side.

Wilbur hung on tightly.

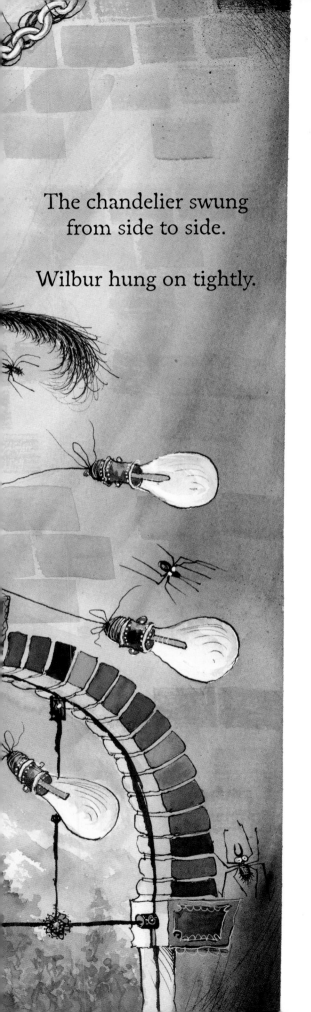

Perhaps the chandelier
wasn't a good idea.

Wilbur jumped back onto
the banister just in time.

CRASH!

It definitely wasn't a good idea.

Winnie rushed into the hall.
'My beautiful chandelier!'
she cried. 'My house *is* haunted.
There must be a spell to fix a
haunted house.'

Winnie picked up her Big
Book of Spells and quickly
turned over the pages.
Yes, there it was: a spell for
fixing a haunted house.
Wasn't it?
It was hard to read it
without her glasses.

She shut her eyes,
stamped her foot three times,
waved her magic wand,
and shouted,

'Abracadabra!'

There was a
great gust of wind
and everything went dark.
Owls and bats flew overhead.
Skeletons rattled on the staircases.
Spiders' webs hung from the ceilings,
thick with hairy spiders. Ghosts slithered
through the walls. '**Woo, woo, wooo**,' they cried.
Winnie's house *really* was a haunted house.

Whooosh!

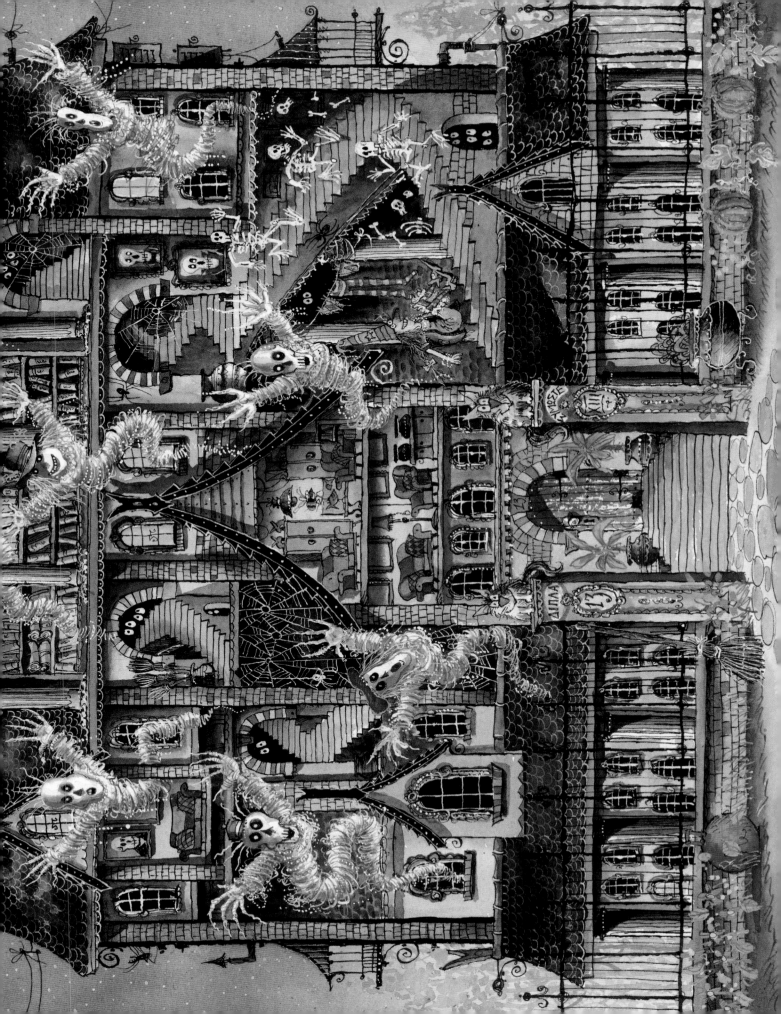

'BOO!'
shouted a ghost.
Winnie was very surprised.

She jumped back,
into a sticky spider's web.

A big hairy spider tickled her nose.

'Urk! Yuck! A-a-a-chooo!'

Wilbur came running down the stairs.
'Meeow, meeeow,' he cried.

'Don't be frightened, Wilbur,'
Winnie said. 'I must have made
a mistake with my spell.'

She looked in the Big Book of Spells again,
and a swooping owl knocked her glasses onto her nose.
'So that's where they were,' she said.
Winnie looked carefully at the spell.

It said:

⚙ To ⚙
★ Make ☾
a Haunted House.

'Oh dear,'
said Winnie.
'I didn't see
to make.'

Winnie looked at the next spell.
It said:

To
FIX
a Haunted House
DO the haunting
spell backwards.

'That should work,'
Winnie said.

She opened her eyes wide,
waved her foot high in the air three times,
waved her wand backwards,
and shouted,

'Arbadacarba!'

WHOOSH!

All was quiet. Winnie's haunted house was
Winnie's house again. But it was a very messy house.

There were bits of vase,
heaps of curtains,
and chunks of chandelier
everywhere.

'Never mind,' Winnie said. 'I'll soon clean it up.'
She waved her magic wand, shouted,

'Abracadabra!'

. . . and the vase, the curtains, and the
chandelier were as good as new.
'That's a very useful spell,' Winnie said.

Then Winnie sat down in an armchair.
She thought she'd finish her sleep.
Wilbur climbed onto her lap.
He really needed a sleep.

'We've had an exciting day, haven't we, Wilbur,'
Winnie said. 'I don't suppose I'll ever know
what *was* haunting my house.'

I hope not, Wilbur thought.
'Purr, purr, purr,' he said.

Bethany

Katia

Eun-Jae

Kathleen

Ji-Eun

Jenny

Sara

Fraser

Ka Keung

Selin

Selin

Olivia

Siyabend

Kieran

A note for grown-ups

Oxford Owl is a FREE and easy-to-use website packed with support and advice about everything to do with reading.

Informative videos

Hints, tips and fun activities

Top tips from top writers for reading with your child

Help with choosing picture books

For this expert advice and much, much more about how children learn to read and how to keep them reading ...

LOOK
for Oxford Owl
www.oxfordowl.co.uk